ICEBERG !

(Hardcover title: High Tide for Labrador)

by EVE BUNTING

illustrated by Bernard Garbutt
cover by Tran Mawicke

SCHOLASTIC BOOK SERVICES

NEW YORK · TORONTO · LONDON · AUCKLAND · SYDNEY · TOKYO

To the memory of Jane

ISBN: 0-590-30880-7

12 11 10 9 8 7 6 5 4 3 2 1   11   9/7 0 1 2 3 4/8

Printed in the U.S.A.   11

Books by Eve Bunting available from Scholastic Book Services:

The Wild One
Iceberg!

1

Big Simon slammed the kitchen door shut and leaned against it. Jimmy looked up from the book he was reading and he knew before the words were spoken.

"It's fixed," Big Simon said. "I talked to Captain Will this morning. Jimmy's signed on the *Kathleen II.*"

Jimmy's mother smiled. She pulled the old cardigan she wore tightly about her, wrapping her arms around herself. Her smile didn't fool Jimmy. She didn't *want* him to go, but she had her reasons, whatever they were, for allowing it.

"Hear that, Jimmy?" She came across to him, ruffled his hair. "Thirteen years old and going out from Newfoundland to fish the Labrador."

1

Jimmy saw the look, the quick, secret look that passed between her and Big Simon, and he felt the same choking rage that always came when he saw them together. He shook his head a little, moving her hand, and bent again over the book. The print on the page ran together like tangled fishing lines.

"Don't you have something to say to Simon?" His mother's voice had a jagged edge to it. "Him putting his name up for you, speaking to Captain Will, making himself responsible for you on the voyage? It's not all the time they're taking a boy along, you know."

"I know." Big Simon's face was suddenly hazy through the mist in Jimmy's eyes and the swirling blue smoke from Big Simon's pipe. "Thank you."

Big Simon nodded. "You'll not be going as a sharesman, mind. The fish you jig yourself will be your own and will be your take for the voyage. You'll work for your grub, but you'll be learning the ways of the Labrador."

"When do you go?" Mrs. Donovan was busying herself folding clothes on the edge of the table and her voice said it didn't matter if it was today or next year. But her voice was lying too.

"Tomorrow, if all goes well. We're waiting for word on the pack ice. There's a plane coming in this morning that'll be able to tell us how it looks. The Captain's itching to be away. With this being his last voyage he's bound he'll get a start on the other boats." He tapped the bowl of his pipe in his hand. "Well, I'll be getting back down there."

Jimmy closed the book. "Wait. I'd best go along with you." He took his plaid jacket and knitted cap from the hook by the door. Standing, he knew again the size of Big Simon. Five seven already himself, he doubted if he'd ever top him. There wasn't a door in Davidstown Big Simon could go through without stooping.

"You'll come back and eat with us, Simon?"

Again Jimmy felt the thrust of the anger inside him. Why did Big Simon have to be with them all the time?

"Aye. I'll come up again with the boy."

They walked together through the town, no words between them. Does he know? Jimmy wondered. Does he know how I hate him? He glanced up quickly at Big Simon's face with its thick, rusty mustache and curling, brick-red hair. The kind of nose and chin you see on a totem pole, blunt and fierce. Ugly, Jimmy thought. What does Mother see in him?

He remembered his father, pulling the memory forward, forcing it from the shadows. Not tall, eyes that laughed, teeth that were square and had small gaps between them. Was he thinking of his father's face or his own in the mirror? He remembered riding on a man's shoulders. There was a sweater, thick and gray, with a pattern of brown reindeer knitted into it. It had smelled of tar. A raveled piece, like a fish's backbone, lay across one sleeve. Strange how the sweater was clearer than anything else.

A sailor he'd been, and a fisherman, but he had died in his bed. Jimmy remembered the drawn blinds and the silence that filled the rooms. People had come from all over, from as far away as St. John's. Everyone knew his father. He remembered his Aunt Cristobel crying, hugging him, and whispering, "The best man that ever lived, your dad. There'll not be another like him." She'd held him away from her, looking at him strangely. "Except maybe you, Jimmy. Aye, maybe you."

He was six then and he and his mother had been alone ever since. There wasn't much money—but soon it would be different. He'd learn the net fishing this summer, and next year he'd go on the *Kathleen II* the same as the rest of them, working for his share. He'd bring home five, maybe six hundred dollars. Then she'd know. She didn't need Big Simon, didn't want Big Simon. Why would she, after his dad? There'd never be another like his dad. Except maybe, except...

Big Simon's voice brought him back to today. They had reached the top of the winding gravel path that led down to the harbor.

"Look at the size of that one, right at the bar mouth." Big Simon pointed out toward the open sea with the stem of his pipe. His hands had freckles on their backs, like the dull spots on a trout's skin. Jimmy's eyes followed the curve of the pipe stem. An iceberg bobbed gently on the water, glistening in the sun. It was big, maybe thirty feet tall, with a hole like an arch in the middle. Through it Jimmy could see the gray of the sea sliding up and down as the berg moved.

"She's come in with the tide," Big Simon said. "It doesn't look good. I'm thinking there'll be a slow breakup this year."

"Will we have to wait?" Jimmy heard the surly note in his own voice that was always there when he spoke to Big Simon.

"Not if Captain Will can help it. We'll nose our way out. Getting to the fishing grounds first makes the difference. Them that does gets the best berths."

Jimmy nodded. He knew that. He'd lived in Davidstown all his life and he'd seen the boats set out for the Labrador every May, one or two of them always sneaking away before sunup. He knew plenty about boats and fishing and the ways of the sea, although he'd never been on a voyage. Big Simon didn't have to explain to him.

The Kathleen II was tied to a hawser. An old diesel-motor fishing boat, she sat high in the water, stubby and sturdy, built for her job of hauling and carrying the big cod and the men who caught them. Nets, like giant cobwebs, shimmered her decks.

Jimmy held his breath, feeling the stirring inside that always came to him with the smell of the salt and the fish and the old, crusty ropes. A boat, getting ready to go out for the Labrador, and this time he'd be on her.

"She's a good boat with a good captain," Big Simon said, and Jimmy pushed his excitement into the back of his head. There wasn't anything he wanted to share with Big Simon.

6

The dock hummed with movement. Jimmy saw Michael Moore and Slim Crawford rolling the big oil drums onto the deck. One of the Laidlaw brothers was busy filling water barrels from a snake of a hose that stretched across a pile of lumber and somebody's old stove-in dinghy. Sacks of flour and potatoes waited to be loaded. There were cartons of condensed milk and cans of coffee and fruit.

Again the joy bubbled in him. He was going. Tomorrow, the day after, soon. His voice was flat. "I'd best get to it, lend a hand."

"Aye."

He ran down the rutted path toward the boat. *He* doesn't know what I'm thinking, he thought exultantly. He doesn't know if I want to go or not, if I'm happy or scared, or what. He knows nothing about me, for I've shown him nothing.

He stopped as the thought hit him. And he's shown me nothing. I know nothing about him either.

2

It was early morning, two days later, when they left. There were a few women and boys on the dock, waving, but there were no crowds to see them away. This was work and it happened at the beginning of every summer. The men were going out for the Labrador.

The big berg floated lazily at the mouth of the harbor and they steered well clear of it. From a hundred yards Jimmy could see its jagged edges, sharp as icepicks. Many a good ship had gone down, pierced by ice like that. Jimmy shivered. He'd heard stories, lots of stories.

There was a gentle swell on the open sea and the *Kathleen II*, her holds empty, rolled with the swell. Bits of broken pack ice dotted the water, white and soft as eider ducks.

Jimmy watched the houses and the harbor grow smaller and smaller. He warmed his hands around his mug of hot cocoa and tried not to think of his mother standing in the doorway where he had left her. She'd had her hair in two braids that hung down over her shoulders and she'd looked like a little girl. Don't think about her, he warned himself, think about the voyage.

The shore had disappeared. Out here the pack ice was heavier. Jimmy watched a big piece that rolled on the sea like a surfaced whale. A Beluga whale, white and sleek and shiny.

Behind the *Kathleen II* the ship's boat hissed through the water, taut on the end of its tow rope.

He sat down, his back against a coil of oily rope, and closed his eyes. There wouldn't be much for him to do until the fishing began.

"You'll be expected to work for your voyage," Captain Will had said. "There'll be the innards to scrub and the tongues to come out, and you'll be cutting pairs of cod cheeks. If you don't know how, you can learn. When you've time of your own you can jig for yourself."

Jimmy had nodded. He'd learn. Captain Will needn't worry.

"Ice fog coming in!" The lookout's voice was

loud and clear over the chug-chug of the engine. "Coming thick and heavy!"

Jimmy leaned over the rail and looked ahead. Fog was a shifting gray ghost that closed silently across the water. There was a whiteness, a gleaming bulk that showed itself momentarily in the line where sea met fog.

"Growler in the water off the starboard bow," the lookout called and Jimmy heard the helmsman bark an answer. The engine sound slowed a beat.

He made his way to the wheelhouse, pushing between the lashed-down water barrels and two up-ended dories.

The wheelhouse was filled with warmth and pipe smoke and the crackling of the radio. Captain Will hunched over the ship-to-shore speaker.

"Belle Isle, Belle Isle." The radio voice splintered the quiet. "Calling *Kathleen II*, calling *Kathleen II*. Visibility Zero Zero. Pack ice heavy. Visibility Zero Zero."

Captain Will flipped a switch. "*Kathleen II* calling Belle Isle. Message received. We'll head for Saint Anthony. Lie low for a time. Repeat. *Kathleen II* heading for Saint Anthony."

Jimmy saw Big Simon's nod. "Hello, Jimmy. Get your gear stored?"

"Aye. It's stored." Jimmy edged out and closed the door behind him. He had his gear in the cabin he was to share with Michael Moore and Eb

10

Laidlaw. At the last minute his mother had given him the tackle box that had been his father's. The chrome diamond jigs were inside, and a hook big enough to haul a shark, and the lines, coiled neatly the way his father had left them. He had pushed the box under the wooden bunk along with the green duffel bag, and he had tried to push any doubts he had about himself out of sight too. The best fisherman in Davidstown his father had been, maybe the best in Newfoundland. Not many like him around anymore — except maybe his son, Jimmy, his only son, Jimmy.

On deck it was cold and damp. The air seemed dead. Water beaded the railings and darkened the planking of the deck, and the boat was wrapped in a gray fog blanket, suffocating as smoke. The wail of the foghorn echoed off the ocean, smothering in the thickness around them. The *Kathleen II* had slowed almost to a stop.

"Hard to port — pack ice. Hard to port," the lookout called, and the *Kathleen II* churned slowly around.

Big Simon was a shadow beside him. "Nothing to worry about, boy. We're only a few miles from Saint Anthony's."

"Who said I was worried?"

Big Simon shrugged. "Being as how it's your first voyage nobody'd be —"

11

"Berg! Berg to starboard!" The lookout's voice was sharp as flint.

The foghorn moaned three times and the men came tumbling out on deck.

Jimmy hadn't noticed the poles fastened upright to the bulkheads, but now he saw the men pulling them free, running with them to the rail on the starboard side. The engine throb was loud and the *Kathleen II* shuddered and shook. Then, out of the fog, he saw the iceberg.

It towered over the boat, so close that he felt he could put out a hand and touch the blue-white sides of it. Everything seemed to stand still and there was a clarity in spite of the swirling fog. Jimmy saw every ice grain, every packed particle that made up the whole. There was a dent in front, like a giant thumbprint. Bird droppings streaked one side with gray and black lines. It was moving, sliding, gliding straight for the boat.

Fear was suddenly a thick bitterness in his throat. They were going to crash. The *Kathleen II* surged to port, her engines growling as she tried to pick up speed. Her stern swung around. That's where they would hit. He thought about it calmly. There would be a creaking, a grinding, a rending of timbers, and then the whole back end would be shorn away as a cleaver whacks the tail off a cod. She'd go down by the stern. How long would they stay afloat? She'd fill up fast. A few

12

miles from Saint Anthony's — too far — no way to make it.

"Grab something, Jimmy! Push!"

His whole being had been fastened on the berg so that everything around him had faded into the fog. Now he saw, as if from some great distance, that every man on the boat was leaning across the starboard railing toward the stern. They had the poles and they were pushing the iceberg, holding it away from its advance on the boat. They strained and shoved. The muscles on their necks and arms stood out like knots on a rope. The berg dwarfed them. They were ants pushing against a chunk of limestone.

The *Kathleen II* tipped to one side, her decks slanting from the crew's weight, and, as Jimmy stood fixed with fear, it seemed she was bound to go down to starboard before she hit. Poles snapped and men grabbed oars and deck scrubbers and metal-poled gaff hooks to hold the ice away.

There was a sucking noise, a swirl of water, and then a crash, loud as summer thunder. For a few seconds it sounded as if someone were crunching a giant crab shell. The berg had smashed the ship's boat, snapping it in two. It carried half of the boat with it, pushing it ahead in the water. But the *Kathleen II* had cleared.

The men sat where they had stood. They panted and grunted and didn't look at one another.

"Lost the goldarn ship's boat," somebody muttered.

"Better than us."

"Goldarn right. And we still have the dories. Did you see the size of that thing? Must have calved off a bigger one still, or she'd be spread out more under the water. Could have cut us clean in half."

The foghorn moaned. Slowly the men began to move around, standing and stretching, putting the poles back against the bulkhead, shoving the oars again under the dories.

"Hey! Where were you when the rest of us were pushing our guts out?" Michael Moore glared at Jimmy. "You're a part of this crew, you know. You ain't no paying passenger!"

Jimmy felt all heads turn toward him and he wanted to crawl away somewhere and be sick, all by himself.

"Leave him alone, Moore." It was Big Simon's voice. "I mind well your first voyage when you caught your thumb on a barb hook and fainted dead away. And you older than the boy here by a good five years."

Michael Moore scowled, but the men laughed. The danger was over and the laughter was louder than it might have been. Under its cover Jimmy edged away. He felt tears, hot in his eyes. Where *had* he been? Standing like a rat cornered in a hold, watching the others save the ship. Just like his dad! Sure he was! Just like his dad.

He huddled against the sloping wall of the wheelhouse, hugging his misery. Bad enough that he had been scared out of his wits, but to have Big Simon see it and defend him — that was worse than anything.

15

3

They reached Saint Anthony in less than an hour, the fog lightening the closer they got to shore. As they chugged into the harbor, streamers of mist waved harmlessly, like banners from their masts.

The day was spent taking on salt, pouring it in bagfuls down the metal chutes into containers in the holds. The crystals glittered like powered snow and Jimmy thought again of the big berg and the horror of waiting for it to hit. He shivered.

"That seems like a lot of salt," he said to Slim Crawford, speaking quickly to take his mind from the thoughts that crowded it.

"We'll haul a lot of fish." Slim opened another

sack and filled the chute again. "It takes a pound of salt for a pound and a half of cod. If we don't carry enough we might just as well throw the fish back. They'll spoil before we get them home." Slim's voice held no reminder that Jimmy had been scared. All the men of the *Kathleen II* were full of jokes and laughter. Maybe, Jimmy thought, it was always that way when death came close without grabbing.

He tried to make up some by working extra-hard, carrying the heavy sacks, emptying them time and again into the darkness below.

"Take it easy now, Jimmy. There's herrings cooking and a boy needs his grub if he's to grow." Big Simon put his foot on the sack Jimmy was about to lift and Jimmy straightened, feeling the tiredness in his back and arms. "Moore'll do some work for a change," Big Simon added. "He's getting wearied, clocking there on that water barrel, watching others do the loading."

"Aye, aye, Captain sir, Boss Man!" Mike Moore's voice was sarcastic and he gave Simon a cold look. "Sounds like you're jumping the starting gun." He spoke softly as he passed Jimmy. "Poor Mama's boy! Mama's boy needing a rest?"

Jimmy felt heat in his face. Why did Big Simon always treat him like a youngster in front of the men? "Sit where you were, Moore," he said. "I'll finish what I started."

"It's up to you." Big Simon turned his back and Jimmy saw Mike Moore's sly grin and knew he'd been shamed into doing more than his share.

Captain Will pulled Jimmy's hair as he went by. "I see I've got me a good hand here," he said. "Better than those good-for-nothings!" He nodded to where a group of the men sat playing cards with the crew from the *Daughter Dear*. But Captain Will's scowl held nothing of anger. He strutted along the dock on his short thick legs, bantering with everyone he met. He and his ship and his crew were safe, and they had as good a chance as anyone of getting to the fishing grounds first.

Everything had stopped. Saint Anthony's harbor was choked with fishing boats of all builds and sizes. There was even an old two-masted schooner, still graceful and beautiful. Slim Crawford said she was on her last voyage to the Labrador, like Captain Will himself.

The pack was bad and none of them dared venture out, what with the radios reporting ice from Nain to the Belle Isle Straits. So they waited.

For three days they waited. On the third night the forecast was better, and on the morning of the fourth day Jimmy woke to the clank of the anchor chain and the beat of the engines. The *Kathleen II* was readying for the Labrador.

He got dressed quickly and went topside. They were poking their way through the ice, the look-

out calling the sea conditions every few minutes.

Jimmy saw Big Simon by the rail and he went the other way so he wouldn't have to pass by him. He'll probably ask me if I took my vitamins, Jimmy thought, or if I'm warm enough nights. He spat toward the sea, the way he saw the men do when they were disgusted.

The radio was growling in the wheelhouse as he slipped inside. The smoky warmth was filled with so much static that it made his ears ache.

Captain Will wiped the steam from the glass with the sleeve of his sweater and peered ahead.

"Not a sight or a sound of the *Queensland*," he muttered, "nor the *Daughter Dear*, either." He turned and saw Jimmy. "Dratted boats slipped out afore sunup." He beckoned with a finger, thick and red as a sausage. "Come on up here and take a look at what's ahead."

Jimmy stood beside him. Small floating islands of ice bumped one another, sliding under water, reappearing. A growler, blue-green, veined and smooth as marble, slipped silently past. In front of the ship's bows was a dark open stream.

"See that point of land way ahead?"

A gray bulk lay like a shadow on the horizon.

"That's the Labrador, Jimmy boy. We'll be through the Straits and coming up on her before the day's over."

Jimmy felt a stirring, deep inside. The land he'd heard of all his life. The waters his father had fished, the waters that turned boys into fishermen. If the boys had it in them...

Captain Will's voice was soft and it was as though he knew Jimmy's thoughts. "I liked your father, Jimmy. We went on three voyages together and one of them was a bad one to the Banks. I had a lot of respect for him. And you have the looks of him about you, and the ways of him, too. It was as much that as Big Simon's word that made me take you along."

Jimmy swallowed, nodded. "Aye." Warmth filled him. "How long will it take us to get to the berths, Captain Will?"

"I reckon eleven, twelve more days, son. We'll be lucky to make thirty miles a day in this ice."

Captain Will's reckoning was good. They did twenty-eight that day, twenty the next, and twenty-two the day after. The lookout needed changing every hour, and the helmsman, too, and tempers were on edge.

Topi Laidlaw threw a whole pan of bread at César, the Portuguese cook, claiming it was burned and tasted like dried seaweed.

Mike Moore prowled around the boat looking for trouble. One day he told Jimmy they were a man short because of him. "We carry eighteen," he said. "This voyage it's seventeen and you. That means less fish for the sharing."

"Aye, and one less to share them with," Jimmy said quickly.

It was the next day that Mike Moore told Jimmy that César had made him "the soup of sorrow." All men who fished the Labrador drank it, he said, for that way you knew for sure you'd be back again to fish these waters. That way you knew for sure you were a seaman.

When César set the soup bowl in front of Jimmy, all the crew gathered to watch. The bowl was filled with fish heads, glassy-eyed, floating in a greasy gray scum. Entrails, fat and yellow, waved like worms under the surface.

Jimmy's stomach heaved at the sight and the

smell. He picked up the spoon, knowing all eyes in the cabin were on him, imagining all the dead eyes in the bowl on him too.

"Sup it up, there's more in the pot," Mike Moore said. He leaned across the table, rubbing his hands, smacking his lips. "It'll put barnacles on your chest and cockles on your muscles."

Jimmy closed his eyes and tried to close his nose. A fish head came up on the first spoonful. He tipped it off and managed to get the liquid into his mouth without gagging. The second spoonful left a thick, pasty stickiness on the roof of his mouth. He quickly drank some more. Don't think, he told himself. Get it down. Don't think about what's in it.

Something slimy trailed over his tongue and a rush of sickness gushed from his stomach to his throat. He lunged from the table, his hand slapped across his mouth. As he retched into the lavatory pot he heard their laughter. His face in the mirror was green, his eyes streaming.

"C'mon, Jimmy boy, soup's getting cold." Mike Moore pushed him again toward the table with a hand on the back of his neck.

"I can't."

"Sure you can." Mike Moore held a spoonful to Jimmy's mouth. Grease had congealed on a yellow stringy thing that wavered on the end of the spoon.

"Open your mouth, close your eyes — "

A spasm of dry retching seized him.

"He's had enough, fellows." It was Big Simon's voice, a smile in it, but an authority there too. "Leave him be."

"You leave *us* be." Mike Moore dropped the spoon with a clatter. "This is none of your business."

"The boy *is* my business." Again Big Simon's voice was light, but he had a way with him that stopped arguments before they began.

Jimmy picked up the spoon. Why was *he* Big Simon's business? "Just because you're a friend of my mother's... " he began, but he didn't know how to finish. He filled the spoon and lifted it shakily to his mouth. He'd show them. He didn't need special treatment, or Big Simon's help, or anything else. The spoon wavered. However hard he willed it, his mouth wouldn't open.

"Suit yourself, Jim," Big Simon said gently. "One thing, though. Those aren't fish guts in the bowl. It's macaroni. But don't eat the heads. They're heads all right — and dead a while by the smell of them."

Jimmy kept his eyes on the shaky spoon until the door closed behind Big Simon. There was total silence in the cabin. He dropped the spoon, pushed back the chair, and ran. He hated them all, but most of all he hated Big Simon, with his protection and his matter-of-fact ways. Why was he always there at the wrong time? Big know-it-all, he thought, and he said it over and over to himself. Big know-it-all. You're not my father, you're not my anything! All at once he began to feel better. He'd have finished the soup if know-it-all had left him alone.

Lying in his bunk that night, he decided that for the rest of the voyage he wouldn't look at Big Simon, wouldn't talk to him, wouldn't answer if Big Simon spoke to him. He wished he could ignore Mike Moore too, but since they shared quarters it wasn't easy. He tried, though, pretending it was only Eb Laidlaw in the cabin, whistling when Mike Moore made his sarcastic remarks about Mama's Boy as if he didn't hear them.

Each night he took out the tackle box. He felt the points on the big barb, weighed the jigs in the palm of his hand, and let the line slip through his fingers. He imagined his father on a voyage like this, waiting for the work to start, and his throat ached. He wasn't sure if it ached for his father, then, or if it ached for Jimmy, now.

They were nearly a fortnight out of Newfoundland and the men's spirits brightened. Soon now, soon.

On the fifteenth day Jimmy went to the wheelhouse.

"Tomorrow we'll be hauling them in and throwing them on board," Captain Will said. He winked happily at Jimmy. "How's about that, boy?"

Big Simon stood with his back to the wheelhouse stove. His nod to Jimmy was friendly.

"I'm wondering where the *Queensland*'s got to …" Captain Will began. The crackling of the radio interrupted him.

"All boats, all boats…this is Goose Bay." There was an urgency to the words. "Make for nearest harbor. Heavy pack moving in with the tide. Leads closing. Repeat, leads closing."

Captain Will grabbed the radio mike and flipped the switch.

"*Kathleen II,* message received. What news of the *Daughter Dear* and the trawler *Queensland?* Advise if you know their position."

The voice was fainter. "*Daughter Dear* and *Queensland* safe in McKenzie Inlet. Repeat. All boats make for nearest…" The static took over, whistling and growling.

Captain Will fiddled with the dials and then turned the radio off. He stood, rubbing the short gray stubble on his chin. "Leads closing," he said. "And the two of them in McKenzie already. That's barely two miles from the fishing grounds. They took the other side of the island, beat us to it." He raised the binoculars, sweeping them in all directions across the sea. "Here, Simon, have a look."

Big Simon moved the glasses slowly. "If we're

caught in the ice we'll be smashed like a nut in a nutcracker," he said at last. "Do you remember the *Curley*? They were lucky to get the crew off."

"Aye. And it's closing fast." Captain Will's voice was so low he might have been talking to himself. "But if we don't take a tolerable cargo the men won't eat this winter." He took the glasses again and polished their lenses on the sleeve of his sweater. "Simon! If the *Queensland* gets there ahead of us she'll scoop it clean and we'll be hauling nets full of water."

They stood, not looking at one another.

"It's your decision," Big Simon said at last. "You're still captain."

"Aye."

The helm was changing. The new helmsman repeated the course as he took over the steering. He looked once at the Captain.

"Steady as she goes," Captain Will said. All Jimmy could see of him was his back, the shoulders hunched under the thick sweater. The decision had been made. The *Kathleen II* steamed on.

4

The leads were closing. The *Kathleen II* swung in and out, searching for open water.

"Hard-a-starboard . . . steady . . . steady . . . port easy."

Now the sea was a sea of ice, and a frozen wind tumbled the low growlers over and over in the water. It was hard to tell what was ice and what was a whitecap, whipped by the wind.

The men crowded the railings, the poles in their hands.

"Ice ahead, ice ahead," the lookout's voice intoned monotonously.

Sometimes there would be the cry, "Ring her down," and the engine would slow and stop. When the engine noise died, Jimmy could hear the grinding of the ice floes, the squeaking as they rubbed together. Sometimes the *Kathleen II* would reverse, trying another ribbon of black water. It was like a maze, Jimmy thought. One of the kind that used to be in the puzzle part of the Sunday paper. At the end, if they found the way out, was the prize.

They hugged the shore, barely a quarter-mile from the bleak, black cliffs, the ice pushing them closer and closer as it moved with the incoming tide.

César, the cook, came up from below and gave Jimmy mugs of hot coffee to take to the wheelhouse. Big Simon and Captain Will took the thick cups without looking away from the sea ahead.

"If we make McKenzie we'll have near as good a chance as they do." Jimmy had to admit that there was a sort of comfort in Big Simon's steady, strong voice.

Captain Will's eyes were red and tired and he rubbed at them with the palm of his hand. "The *Queensland*'s faster than us by a good three knots," he said. He drank, coughed. "But aye, if we get to McKenzie we'll have some chance anyways."

It didn't look as if they would ever get to McKenzie. The *Kathleen II* moved at a rower's pace.

Jimmy left the wheelhouse and stood at the

rails with the men. He had found himself a piece of planking and he half-hoped for the chance to fend off with it. This time he'd be ready.

The cold was lip splitting, ear burning. The sea was a deep dark green, the color of bottle glass. Close, so close to the cliffs that Jimmy could see the nests of the crowbills high on the ledges and hear their harsh cries. Waves built themselves and threw their force against the narrow shingle beaches.

The men were silent. Now and again one would push away a piece of pack ice, bigger than the rest.

"Leastaways there's no fog," somebody said.

"Leastaways not yet," somebody else answered grimly.

Jimmy wondered how it would be when the ice edged them into the breaking surf. Would the *Kathleen II* go aground, the waves pounding her, breaking her? Would she be carried like a piece of driftwood, raised high and flung in pieces on the beach? How deep was her keel? And what about life jackets? He looked around, secretly. There were piles of bright orange preservers under the two dories. Why wasn't anyone wearing one? He wanted to run, fasten one on, but he didn't. Pains gnawed at his stomach and he heard its nervous rumble. The first voyage of Jimmy Donovan, the last voyage of Jimmy Donovan.

The engine seemed to pick up a beat and he felt the ship's bow turn sharply to starboard. They were heading out to sea, away from the cliffs.

The men rushed forward to see what was happening. A narrow lead, no wider than the gravel path that led down to Davidstown harbor, had opened to starboard. The *Kathleen II* pushed her way through it, her prow the narrow edge of the wedge that parted the ice floes before them. There was a blunt black headland that stuck into the ocean. The boat was edging out and around it.

"By Christmas we're going to make it," Slim Crawford whispered. "McKenzie's on the other side. The old Captain's pulled us through."

But they weren't through yet. It took almost an hour to round the point, ice crackling and breaking against their hull, the boat stopping and reversing, but stubbornly butting its way on. When they turned the headland they saw the inlet and the two ships lying in it.

"We'll be all right now," Topi Laidlaw said, slapping Jimmy on the back. "The inlet turns, you see, so it's against the tide. The ice drifts past its mouth. The fishes won't have us this time!"

Jimmy unclenched his hands from the rail. He had to use his mind hard to pry them off. They were stuck fast, like barnacles on a rock, and his fingers ached from the tightness of his grip. They were safe. The fishes wouldn't have them.

He read the names of the boats in the inlet — the *Daughter Dear* and the *Queensland*. Their decks were lined with men and they waved to the *Kathleen II* as she anchored between them and the mouth of the inlet. The captain of the *Queensland* shouted across.

"Rough going out there, Captain Will."

"Aye," Captain Will said, and Jimmy didn't know if it was spray or sweat that he wiped from his brow.

"There's no flies on us," someone yelled from the *Kathleen II*. "We be sailors on this old tub."

Now the boat was noisy and cheery as they dropped anchor. Everyone was talking at once and Jimmy found he was beginning to understand. Like his own clenched fists, the men held tight and only let go when the danger was over.

César outdid himself at dinnertime. There were two smoked hams and they had them with boiled potatoes and canned greens. Captain Will opened five bottles of red wine and they toasted the *Kathleen II* and Captain Will and all those fat prime cod lying on the bottom of the ocean, waiting to be caught. It was a good night and Jimmy felt himself a part of the crew. Hadn't he gone through the dangers with the rest of them? He was glad he hadn't rushed for a life jacket — and, after all, nobody knew about the pains in his stomach but himself. He joined in the singing and pretended he didn't hear when Mike Moore told him he was a good soprano.

After they had eaten and drunk their fill, Captain Will rapped his spoon on his glass and called for quiet.

"We'll man three watches tonight," he said. "Two men, changing every three hours. I'm running no risk of the *Daughter Dear* or the *Queensland* slipping out ahead of us. The skies are clear, there's a moon, nobody's going anywheres without our knowing it." He stopped. "We're almost there, men. Two more miles, that's all it is."

The men twirled their glasses and puffed smoke from their pipes. "Tomorrow it may be, or the day after, God willing."

There was the stamp of feet and the roar of approval.

The first watch was set and the rest of them rolled into their bunks. Jimmy felt the gentle, friendly tug of the *Kathleen II* at her anchor. He listened hard and it seemed to him he could hear the clash of the ice in the open sea, but maybe it was the remembered clashing in his mind and nowhere else. He felt under the bunk and brought out the tackle box.

Michael Moore's voice was soft through the darkness. "Your daddy's, was it? Well, never mind now. I hear tell you're getting yourself a new daddy, a live one who'll take care of Mama's Boy. Mama's Boy won't have to worry no more." He sniggered. "Mama won't have to worry no more, either."

Jimmy leaped out of the bunk and across the slope of the floor. He lunged at that bulk that was Mike Moore, throwing himself on top of it, kicking and pounding.

"*Shut up, shut up, shut up!*" he yelled, and there was a redness in his eyes and he could have gone on kicking and fighting until he collapsed.

Eb Laidlaw hauled him off by the hair. "Cut it out, Donovan. Captain Will won't stand for fighting on his ship. You cut it out, you hear?"

He flung Jimmy back on his own bunk.

Mike Moore's face was a white blur in the shadows. "Donovan, you'll be sorry. I promise you."

Jimmy saw him sit up, rubbing his jaw.

"Give over, Moore. You started it, if not with your fists with your mouth." Eb Laidlaw rolled back in his own bunk. "Jimmy and me have the second watch. We need our sleep. You can settle any grievance you have with him when the voyage is over."

"I'll settle it all right."

Jimmy lay very still. The anger had drained from him as quickly as it had come. What did Mike Moore know? Was his mother for sure to marry Big Simon? Had she forgotten his father, thrown the memory of him away like an old bucket of bait? He buried his head under the rough blankets and fought back tears. *Mama's Boy!* Was that what he was? Had she sent him on the voyage to toughen him up? Had she asked Big Simon to look out for him, make sure he didn't get hurt? The tears hardened, became gravel in his eyes.

He came from under the blankets. Michael Moore and Eb were both snoring when he got out of his bunk. He dressed in heavy trousers and his plaid jacket and went up through the sleeping boat.

Moonlight whitened the deck and spilled in creases on the sea. The *Daughter Dear* and the *Queensland* lay joined to their own reflections on the dark water. The starboard watch sat on a packing case, smoking a cigarette.

One of the dories was gone from the deck. Jimmy sat in the shadow of the other one, looking up at the sky and the black cliffs. What if he ran away after the voyage? A new father! Mama's Boy! The words chased one another in and out of his mind. The cold made his eyes ache.

There was a faint splash of oars and he saw the starboard watch move to the railing. Voices, and Jimmy recognized Captain Will's and Big Simon's. There was a scuffing sound, quiet cursing. Then the lookout was giving Captain Will a hand up and onto the deck. Big Simon followed and Jimmy guessed the two of them had been out in the dory, scouting around. Big Simon looked gigantic, outlined against the lightness of the sky.

"A dory might get through," Captain Will said.

Jimmy saw Big Simon shake his head. "There would have to be only one man in it. We had less than a foot of freeboard and we had no trap lines."

"And we weren't in the open sea." Captain Will blew on his hands. He turned his back to the railing and looked up at the cliffs. Jimmy crouched back in the shadows.

"If there was only some way to scale those

things and go overland," Captain Will said. "They're slicker than an eel's belly. Not a hand-hold or a toehold from top to bottom." He turned back toward the sea.

They stood silently.

"I'll take the dory and try it," Big Simon said at last. "With everything going for me I could make it."

"No. You're too big, too heavy." The Captain stopped. "How about Moore? He's the smallest of the crew."

Big Simon grunted. "You know the saying, 'One hand for the boat, the other for me'? Moore doesn't know about the one for the boat. Why did you bring him, anyways? He's always been a troublemaker."

"He's the best splitter in Newfoundland. Split-ters aren't easy come by." Captain Will lit his pipe and Jimmy saw the red glow of it, brightening and fading as he puffed.

"He'll not come on the voyage next year," Big Simon said. "I'll find me another."

Jimmy sat straighter. *He'd* find another?

Big Simon was talking again. "He wasn't with us last summer. He wouldn't know where to set the traps."

"He'd be easy enough told. The base of Eagle Rock on the west. There's no way he could miss that. You mind one of the Laidlaws painted a big yellow eye on it last year? The lean-to on the east, and then straight into the water as far as the trap lines would stretch." The pipe sent a sparkle of scarlet into the sky. "He could do it in two hours, maybe less. Hug the coast. Be there afore sunup. Take grub and water and blankets with him. There's the lean-to and plenty of wood around for a fire. We'll be there ourselves in a day or two."

Big Simon scratched his head. "It's a risk, Captain. I don't know if Moore has the gut, or the savvy either. What if he can't get through? What if he can't get back?"

Jimmy heard the small plop-plop of the dory bumping the sides of the *Kathleen II*. The big boat creaked and groaned at her mooring.

Captain Will straightened. "Aye. I've never gambled a life yet and I don't guess I aim to do it now. We'll take our chances in a race with the other two and we'll get there first. I don't know how, but some way. We have to." He pulled up the collar of his pea jacket. "I'd have liked it fine if my last voyage had been a good one, Simon. Call me a vain old man and it'd be the truth."

Jimmy saw Big Simon put his arm across Captain Will's shoulders. They called their good nights to the watch, then passed so close that he could see the mists of their breathing hanging before their faces. He listened as their footsteps died away.

Then he sat, huddled in his own heat, thinking. Thinking of the sea outside the inlet, heavy with ice. Thinking of the emptiness and the white movement of it. Two hours. Just two hours. He'd seen trap lines set plenty of times. There was nothing to it.

"Seventeen men and you," Mike Moore had said and his lip had curled in the saying. What if he could save the voyage for all of them? Captain Will's last voyage. Captain Will who had sailed with his father before Jimmy was born. "You have the looks of him, Jimmy, and the ways of him." And Big Simon, what would he think? And his mother...?

Two hours, just two hours. He was small, as small as Mike Moore, and he had the savvy and the gut. He shivered. Didn't he? *Didn't he?*

5

He sat in the chill of the moonlight, making plans. He'd need food. That part would be easy.

Old John Taylor, the port watch, was sitting with his back to the wheelhouse, squeezing his concertina. He grinned when he saw Jimmy heading for the galley.

"I always had the hunger in me when I was a boy. Stoke up a bit before you come on watch. It's colder than a Polar Bear's nose out here."

Jimmy nodded. "I aim to."

He found cheese, dried apples, and the leavings of the smoked hams in the galley. A plastic bottle that had once held laundry bleach made a good water container. A box of matches — two boxes, just in case. There was a big black rubber flashlight hanging on a hook by the door and he took that too. He put everything in a potato sack and carried it topside.

Old Taylor was singing to himself, his back to Jimmy.

> *The codfish lays a million eggs,*
> *The homely hen lays one,*
> *But the codfish never cackles*
> *To tell you what she's done.*

Jimmy jammed the sack between a water barrel and the ship's rail, out of sight. Back down in the cabin, he wrapped his father's tackle box in the two gray blankets off his bunk, carried it on deck and put it with the sack. He stood for a minute, looking across the inlet, listening to Old Taylor at his singing.

> *Ye finny monsters of the deep,*
> *Lift up your heads and shout!*
> *Ye codfish, from your hollows creep*
> *And wag your tails about!*

Out there were the rich fishing grounds, the cod waiting to be lifted — and it was first come, first served. Jimmy shivered. What would happen if he failed? He remembered winters in Davidstown when the summer catch had been poor. The long hungry lines outside the Welfare, the bad days, with the men surly, the women anxious. He wouldn't fail, he *couldn't*!

A seal swam silently by, sleek and shining, its shadow darker than the water above and below it. It glided around the *Kathleen II* as though in answer to the music, and he saw the ripple of its flippers as it turned on its back.

Time was passing. It must be near midnight.

Down below, he pulled a heavy sweater on under his jacket and another pair of socks under his thigh-high boots. There was nothing more to be done. He sat on the edge of the bunk and fear hit him like a blow to the stomach. What was he doing? Why?

There was a thump on the door and a voice shouted, "Laidlaw! Donovan! Your watch." Eb grunted and turned over. When Jimmy shook his shoulder he blinked and sat up. "You dressed already?"

"I couldn't sleep."

Mike Moore opened his eyes and yawned. "Take good care of Mama's Boy, Eb. Don't let the monsters get him. You do and Big Simon'll get *you*. Besides, I have plans for Mama's Boy myself, later."

"Shut up, Moore," Eb said mechanically. He sat on his bunk and began dragging on his clothes.

Jimmy felt anger warming him again and he

was glad of it for it left no room for fear. He looked at Mike Moore and it was all he could do to keep quiet. Mama's Boy was going. Going to do what Big Simon said Moore didn't have the gut for. Big Simon was no fool, come to think of it. A know-it-all, but no fool.

"You want port or starboard?" Eb asked as they climbed topside.

Jimmy shrugged. "Makes no difference." But he turned right at the wheelhouse to the side where the dory bobbed and the supplies were hidden.

"Keep your eyes open now." Eb pulled back his sleeve and looked at the luminous dial on his wrist. "I'll come for you when our watch is over."

"I'll be here," Jimmy said, not thinking and not meaning to lie. He waited a few minutes after Eb had gone, searching the dark, still water for movement or sound. There was none. From here he could see neither the *Daughter Dear* nor the *Queensland*. Only the moon-lightened water shivering toward the open sea.

The trap lines and nets were bulky and awkward. He had trouble sliding them across the deck and over the railing. Little by little he lowered them into the dory below. The cork floats thud-thudded against the hull of the *Kathleen II* on the way down and he held his breath. But no one came to see what was happening. The day had been long and the sleep was sound.

He set the tackle box on the deck and dropped the blankets next. They fell soundlessly and made a cushion for the dull thump of the potato sack.

Someone coughed. He swung around, his back to the railing, the tackle box hidden behind his legs.

Eb Laidlaw came out of the shadows.

"Donovan? I thought I heard something."

Jimmy grinned. "Naw. It's the dory bumping against the hull. The Captain was out in her earlier. I came over to have a look myself."

For a second he thought Eb was coming across to make sure, but he hesitated and turned back.

"Okay. Just checking," he said.

Jimmy slumped against the rail. Checking on Mama's Boy, he thought. Sure. You gotta watch Mama's Boy.

He peered down at the dory. It lay low in the water already — too low, and he himself still to come. His toe touched the tackle box and he took the belt from his jacket and laced it through the metal handles. He tied the belt around his neck, turning the box so that it rested on his back, just below the shoulders. He'd need both hands going down the ladder. Why was he bringing the box? He didn't know. He only knew he couldn't leave it.

The dory dipped dangerously as he got in, but he steadied it with a hand on the *Kathleen II*. There was no sound anywhere but the slap of water on the hull and the ripple of it against the sides of the dory. He sat, listening, waiting for the thumping of his heart to quiet, but it didn't — and he *had* to *go*. At least a half hour had passed since he and Eb came on watch. Two and a half more and he'd be missed. By then he'd be at the berths with the trap lines nearly set.

He loosened the rope and pushed the dory away from the *Kathleen II*. The black water was frighteningly close to the gunwales, but he figured he had about eight inches of freeboard. If the sea wasn't choppy it would be enough.

He began rowing toward the mouth of the inlet, keeping the *Kathleen II* between the dory and the other two boats. The oars made a gentle splash and he dipped and lifted them carefully, cautiously. From here the *Kathleen II* looked immense. Her mooring lights glowed, warm and friendly in the night. Jimmy swallowed. A good boat and a good captain — but he'd see her again. No need to choke up. And when they next met it would be better. He'd have done something worthwhile. His would be one of the stories the men told when they talked of the Labrador and the men who fished her.

The big dory was heavy, but his arms were

strong and good for the rowing for he'd done plenty of it all his life. In a few minutes he reached the spread of the inlet and rounded the point.

And he saw the sea.

The ice glowed in the moonlight, shining blue-white. Peaks towered over the dory, dwarfing it. The wind had died and there was an eerie sort of calm. The white sky and the white sea were one. And the world was only a blackness of cliffs and a moving whiteness that had no beginning and no end.

Jimmy felt the trembling in his legs. There was nowhere to go, nowhere but back to the inlet where there were men and good boats and safety. He was glad. Let someone else save the voyage. The sea filled him with terror. No need to be ashamed. He had tried and found it impassable.

Then he saw the lead of open water that zig-zagged like a crack at the base of the cliffs and he knew he had to go on. He wiped the sweat from his hands on the legs of his pants and gripped the oars. Northward. Hug the coast. Row, row. He'd make it.

Somewhere behind him as he pulled was Eagle Rock. The cliffs to his right were close, near enough for safety. Row, row. He strained on the oars. Slushy ice gurgled against the blades with a tinkly sound, like cracking the top of the water barrel early on a winter's morning. Row, row. He didn't seem to be moving. Of course he was moving. He pulled again, bracing his feet against a thwart, leaning back so that the leather-wrapped shafts squeaked in the oarlocks. He was still opposite the mouth of the inlet. It was as though he were anchored fast to the bottom.

Fear clawed at him. There was a tightness in his chest and a faraway whining in his ears. A chunk of ice nosed the dory, nudging it gently. Behind it a larger piece moved in.

The inlet! He had to get back to the inlet. If he'd known how it was out here...How could he have known? If he'd known...He swung on one oar, feeling the dory turn in the water, heading back toward the dark opening that was McKenzie Inlet. Was it further away? Row, row, he told himself. Row, row. He looked over his shoulder. Where was it? Where was the inlet? It was at least a hundred yards from him now. He heard a sob like a hiccough and it was himself sobbing. He plunged the oars, feathering the surface, and there was the sharp shock of ice water on his face and hands, and small ice splinters skittered across the bottom of the dory. Easy now, easy, he told himself, and he shipped the oars and looked again over his shoulder.

Ice was closing in, silently, smoothly, between the dory and the shore. He was caught, and he knew suddenly and despairingly what had happened. The tide had turned. The tide that had brought the ice in was moving out to the seething sea, and it was taking him with it.

6

"Help! Help!" His voice was a croak, not the
scream he meant it to be. He used the oar, fend-
ing off the ice, but as fast as he shoved one piece
another piece moved to take its place. The inlet
was farther away now, the heaving, shifting
ice pans stretched in all directions around the
dory. He took deep breaths and tried to stop
shaking. The tide would turn. When it did, it
would carry the pack back toward shore. How
long? How long between tides? Six hours. Six
hours out, six hours in. Surely he could survive
that long.

He spread the trap lines on the bottom planks
of the dory, making a nest in the middle. Then he
curled himself in the two blankets, pulling them

over his head, huddling in his own body heat. Morning will come, he told himself, morning will come. And he found he was saying *please, please, please* in a sort of whimper.

All about him was the sucking, grinding sound of water moving between the ice and under it. Now and then there was the brittle clink of ice edges breaking and crumbling. He took his head from under the covers. He was here, and he could hide from the ice but not from his imagination or his thoughts. Whatever happened to him now, the voyage of the *Kathleen II* was over. If all went well with him, if he got back in, twelve hours would have passed. Too long. The other two boats wouldn't wait that long. Beaten, beaten after all, with the end almost in sight.

He could still see the inlet, a gap in the penciled charcoal of the cliffs. The dory had drifted out and a little northward, and he guessed that a current was helping the tide move the pack. He sat up, gathering the blankets about him. In the far distance, against the strange pallor of the sky, he saw a rock, big and smooth and rounded. An outcropping curved like a beak. Eagle's Rock! He was halfway between it and the inlet now and about two miles out from either. He watched the rock for a few minutes and his throat tightened. How could he have been so stupid as to risk not only his own life, but the whole voyage? Tears stung his eyes. He had wanted to... wanted to what? Wanted to show them. It all seemed so far away now, his reasons so small and petty in the face of what confronted him. Maybe he deserved it, whatever was coming. But Captain Will — he didn't deserve to fail on his last voyage. He'd brought them through the ice and the fog, coaxing the *Kathleen II*, willing them all to safety. It was terrible to think of Captain Will and the men, sleeping peacefully on the boat.

He watched numbly as Eagle Rock moved farther and farther away — except that it was he who was moving, his dory now broadside to the pack, part of it.

Something, somewhere, creaked, groaned. What was it? He looked around, heart scudding, pulse pounding. There it was again, louder beside him. The dory! The dory was being squeezed between two big floes. From somewhere Jimmy remembered the words, Big Simon's words, "Smashed like a nut in a nutcracker." He put his hand against the dory's side timbers and felt them pulse and quiver. She was going to collapse, splinter into a few fragments of board drifting in darkness under the ice. And Jimmy? He saw himself drifting too, his hair swirling like seaweed, his eyes, dead as the fish eyes in the bowl, looking forever up through the cracked glass of the ice.

He stood up quickly. The floe in front of him

was as big as a bedroom floor. He couldn't see its thickness. Would it hold him? The dory quivered. No time to think. He stepped up onto the dory seat and then onto the floe. His weight made it dip and black water sloshed around his boots. He took a few cautious steps toward the middle of the ice. It was rough and hummocky except at the edges and there was an unsteadiness to it — like standing on a raft. He began shivering then, great gulping shudders that tore at him like seasickness.

The creaking sound from the dory had stopped. Should he get back in? Where was he safest?

Then he saw the trap lines. The whole voyage of the *Kathleen II* depended on the nets and he had left them behind. And the blankets and the food and water were in the dory too. He should have brought them with him onto the ice. He couldn't stay alive without them.

He put one foot forward, testing the ice, moving slowly and carefully. Now he was within reach of the dory. He put the weight of both feet on the edge of the ice pan and the edge went under, water sloshing almost to the top of his boots. He was sliding, slipping. Only the gunwales of the dory saved him from falling. He stepped back, his mouth thick with fear. Like a pelican on a piling, he stood frozen until the floe righted itself.

Then he saw what he had done. When the ice pan lowered under his weight, the side of the dory had lifted. Now the flat bottom rested lengthwise along the ice. Could he go out to the edge again, pull the dory up to safety? He licked his lips, tasting the salt of blood where the cold had opened them. If he had the dory he could refloat it when the tide turned, row himself to safety. He took one step forward. The ridges of the soles on his high rubber boots found nothing to grip. He balanced himself, shuffling forward, trying not to think of the way the water was rising halfway to his knees. Now his hands were on the dory. He heaved, leaning backwards as far as he dared.

She came up as though she had been oil-greased, and so fast that he staggered backwards. The sea came up with her, lifting her, floating her crazily across the surface of the floe. He held on, his boots finding a foothold on the hummocky part of the ice. He had it... he had it! And then, with a last surge as the ice settled, the dory slid toward him, riding on a skimming of water. He tried to hold it off, but it was heavier than he knew and it knocked against him. He slipped — and the dory kept coming. It banged against his chest and he was down on the ice on his back, the dory rocking itself to a standstill, his left foot pinned beneath it.

He heard his own cry of pain as the weight crunched on his ankle bone. He put both hands against the side of the dory and pushed. It didn't move. It *must* move. It was on ice. Ice was slippery and the dory bottom was flat. It must move. It didn't. He tried to pull his foot free. It wouldn't come. He felt around him with his hands, and he knew why. The hummocky ice that had given him such traction for pulling had trapped both his feet and the dory. The boat was wedged and would have to be lifted, not slid, and his foot was wedged beneath it.

He pulled frantically then, trying to wriggle his leg out of the high rubber boot. The two pairs of thick socks and the grip on his ankle held him firm. He stopped struggling, lying still, feeling the cold rising from the ice beneath him, his mind threatening to jabber with fear. Think, stay calm, he told himself. Would his body heat melt the ice, melt it enough beneath him so that he could free himself? Could he chip the ice under his leg? The oars! If he had an oar he could lever the boat off. But the oars were on the bottom of the dory. He could remember them there when he shipped them earlier. His thoughts darted like minnows in a jar and he began to scrabble at the ice under his leg, hearing his fingernails slither uselessly over the glassy surface. If the sea would only wash onto the floe one more time, refloat the dory for a single second...

Weakness filled him and he lay back on the ice. Cold, it was so cold. He raised himself on his left elbow, stretching one arm as far as possible into the little boat. The tips of his fingers brushed the rough edge of a blanket. He gripped it weakly between his middle and index fingers, feeling his hand cramp with the effort. He pulled. The blanket moved a fraction of an inch, enough to allow him a proper grip. He pulled again. There was a weight on it. His heart leaped. Maybe an end of an oar? He pulled again, carefully now, and he heard the soft whisper of the blanket along the seat and the heavier slither of something moving with it.

Hand over hand he pulled, willing himself to slowness. There was a small, dull thud as the object, cushioned by the blanket, reached the dory's side. He let himself rest a few seconds, rubbing the elbow that had held his weight. An effort now, an effort. He stretched his arm behind him on the ice, feeling the tug on his leg, gritting his teeth as he swung up and forward in a wide arc as though doing some strange exercise.

His fingers found the blanket and something rougher. He grasped it—lifting, straining to clear the sides of the dory. The potato sack. Food, water, matches, the flashlight! Hope surged. He pulled the blanket down too, putting part of it over him, part underneath him. As he raised up to wedge in the blanket he felt himself sticking to the ice, and he heard the dry, ripping sound as his clothes pulled free. One more time he strained up and forward, his fingers searching inside the dory, but he had taken all he could reach. One blanket...the food. It wasn't much.

He lay back, exhausted. He was so tired, so tired. Under him the floe rocked with the gentle motion of the sea. Would it be bad to sleep a little? He remembered stories of the Greely expedition and Peary's to the Pole. Always the warnings against sleep. But those had been lands right inside the Circle, colder than these, maybe forty, fifty below. Newfoundland was sub-Arctic—Labrador too, wasn't it? He was feeling strangely warm and comfortable. His foot felt numb and there was no pain. Ice pack, he thought, reduces swellings. Good for burns, too, and black eyes. His mother had made an ice pack for his eye the day he fought with Willie Stewart down at the dock. Ice was good for a lot of things.... Mustn't sleep. But those were Polar lands; this was sub-Arctic, wasn't it? His mind tried to focus on the map that hung on the classroom wall. The Isotherm was the one that had the temperatures. Was Centigrade more or less than Fahrenheit? He couldn't remember.

He forced his eyes open. *Mustn't sleep*. The sky and the sea were so big and so white. There was no beginning and no end. Loneliness swept over him as the water had swept over the floe. Marooned. The word tolled in his mind, hollow as a ship's bell. Lonely word. Somebody was crying. Who was it? It was his mother. He was creeping into bed beside her, and it was long ago when he was little and she was crying, small, snuffly sobs. "Lonely, Jimmy. So lonely." Night-crying. But his mother wasn't here. She didn't cry now. When had the crying stopped? When Big Simon came. Yes, when Big Simon came.

Big Simon. He had hair as red as a brick, and hands spattered with freckles. "The boy *is* my business!" Who had said that? Somebody had said that.

Lonely, so lonely. His mind was an empty space swirling with ice fog, but he was warm, so warm and comfortable. The ice was soft, soft as his own bed with its feather mattress. It was his own bed and soon his mother would wake him and it would be morning. It would be morning.

7

It must be morning. "Jimmy!" His mother was calling him. "Jimmy... Jimmy!" But it wasn't his mother's voice, it was Big Simon's, and Jimmy was angry. What was Big Simon doing here so early in the morning? He was always here....

"Jimmy! Jimmy!"

He turned in bed and pulled the blanket over him. There was a wrenching at his leg and he cried out in pain and the pain wakened him. He wasn't in bed. He was on the ice, and he was numb, numb and lifeless. He tried to move, but he couldn't. Was he dead? No, he wasn't. He could see the sky and the stars and the moon. He could see the dory and his own length, like a frozen log on the ice. And he could hear. His heart leaped like a fish in a net. Someone was calling, "Jimmy! Jimmy!" He knew the voice. Big Simon. It *was* Big Simon.

He opened his mouth to cry out, but his lips seemed to be glued together and his cry was a moan. He heard the dull beat of an outboard engine and the shout again. "Jimmy! Jimmy!"

He should do something. He knew he should do something, but it didn't seem worth it. He was so comfortable and so sleepy. Easier to close his eyes and go back into the dream where it was warm and safe and nothing hurt, not even thoughts. He let his eyelids droop. The voice was closer now. There was anger in it and the anger made him open his eyes again.

"Jimmy! You'd better hear me and you'd better answer me. You're somewhere on this ice and I'm going to find you and you're going to help me. I'm not giving up and you're not giving up either."

Big Simon's voice. Something about it. Stops argument before it begins. Simon says jump, we all jump. Simon says shout, we all shout. Simon says, Simon says. He tried again to open his lips, for that was how the game went, and somehow it was important that Big Simon know he hadn't given up. Water! If he could have a drink. His hand moved slowly toward the potato sack. It hurt, it hurt! Needle points stabbed his arm and shoulder. Get the sack...drag it up on his chest.

Heavy...open it...couldn't. His hands were lumps, fat clumsy lumps. He closed his eyes. Too hard...too bad.

"Jimmy Donovan! Goldarn it, man, answer me!"

Simon says, Simon says. There was a despair now in Big Simon's voice, a pleading that Jimmy had never heard before.

He tried again to open the sack, his fingers plucking feebly at the tying—and it was open and he fumbled inside for the water bottle. His hand found the ridged rubber of the flashlight and dragged it out.

He was exhausted now, and there was a pain, like fire in his chest. Find the flashlight button. Somewhere there was a button and if you pushed it the light went on. Wasn't that the way it worked? But the button wouldn't move. He was whimpering soundlessly now. Stupid old flashlight, stupid old flashlight.

"Jimmy!"

Through the haze of his mind he knew that the voice was farther away and he was suddenly aware and terribly afraid. He pushed at the flashlight button with the lumps that were his fingers, using every bit of strength he had left, and he saw the round needle of light stab up toward the sky. His arm didn't belong to him. The flashlight was a weight that he moved from side to side. Why was he doing this? It hurt. It hurt everywhere. It was silly to hurt himself like this. He wasn't going to do this anymore just because someone kept calling his name.

He let his arm fall and the light shone across the ice floe that was his raft, turning it into a transparent sheet of glass, knobby glass full of cracks and flaws. There were patterns, like ferns and stars, buried deep within it. Beautiful! If you folded a piece of paper lengthwise, you could cut out all kinds of things, like stars and dancing men and elephants holding each others tails, or maybe their trunks. Once he'd made a chain of monkeys and his mother had pinned it up over the mantel...

Someone was lifting up his head and holding something to his mouth. Warm liquid ran down his chin. Then his lips were open and he was swallowing, and it was hot and salty and tasted of fish.

"Monkeys over the mantel," he said to Big Simon, and Big Simon nodded and held the thermos of soup again to his lips.

Big Simon lifted the dory from Jimmy's foot as easily as if it had been a paper boat.

Jimmy didn't feel the weight come off his leg. This scared him a little, but not much, for he knew this wasn't Jimmy Donovan, not Jimmy Donovan of Davidstown, Newfoundland, Canada, the World. This was someone else.

Big Simon lifted the someone else and wrapped him in blankets and laid him in the bottom of the dory. There was more of the soup to drink and it was good and hot, and the ice fog was lifting, clearing, drifting out of his head.

Big Simon was a black wedge against the sky.

"This is going to hurt, Jimmy. I want to look at your foot." And Big Simon was pulling off the sea boot and peeling down the socks. Jimmy groaned, for it *was* he, Jimmy Donovan. *His* foot, nobody else's.

Big Simon's voice was soft as butter. "I know, son. It hurts a lot. I can see it does."

Pain was a sickness in his throat as Big Simon's fingers probed the bone.

"Not broken, Jimmy. But it was twisted in the fall and the weight held it like that, wrenched in the socket. Not much swelling."

"Ice pack," Jimmy whispered.

"Aye. You'll not have the use of it for a while." In the slanting beam from the flashlight Jimmy saw Big Simon's face. It *was* like a totem pole, strong and solid. He wondered why he had ever thought it ugly.

Big Simon took a red scarf from the pocket of his pea coat and bound it tightly around Jimmy's ankle. He left the boot off but pulled the socks back on.

There were things Jimmy wanted to say, but

the saying of them wasn't easy. "How did you get here?" he asked instead.

"Came in the other dory. She's pulled up on a floe farther in." Big Simon nodded toward the shore. "I couldn't get any closer so I left the dory when I saw your light. I came over the floes."

Jimmy turned his face away. His voice was muffled. "Over the floes? And you carried blankets?"

"The ice is packed close and my legs are right long."

Jimmy thought about it. The big man jumping across the shifting, moving ice pans, the sea black and treacherous between. He shivered. "Will we be able to get off?"

"Sure." Big Simon sat on the edge of the dory and took his pipe from his pocket. "But not until morning. We'll go back the way I came."

Jimmy's throat tightened with fear. Over the ice? What about his ankle? And the dory with the nets?

A match flared and he saw the pipe bowl glow and darken, and, for an instant, Big Simon's hands with the freckles on the backs. Big Simon would be there. It would be all right. There were things to be said, but the saying of them still wasn't easy.

"How long was it — have I been gone a long time?"

"Eb Laidlaw woke me when he found you gone. But you've been on the ice pan less than an hour. Couldn't have been more or you'd not be alive." Big Simon's voice was matter-of-fact.

"How did you know where to find me?"

Jimmy heard the tap-tapping as Big Simon emptied his pipe, and the sizzle as the hot ash hit the ice.

"Nowhere else you could be, considering the tide and the drift. On the ice, or under it." Big Simon put one long leg over the dory's edge. "Move over, boy. We'll need to share those blankets. There's a couple of hours yet until morning."

He sat, his back against the stern of the dory, the ends of the blankets that covered Jimmy wrapped tightly around his legs. Jimmy felt the heat that came from him, smelled the tobacco and sea smell. There were things to be said, but the saying of them wasn't easy.

"I shouldn't have left my watch," he began. "I shouldn't have taken the nets, risked the whole voyage."

"No, you shouldn't have, but you did. Don't be bothering yourself about it now."

"What about the voyage? We'll not be first now. The best of the fish'll be gone. There'll be less money for the men. Will there be enough... will they have enough to tide them over the winter?" He swallowed, stopped.

"We'll not know that until we see how they're running, Jimmy."

"Captain Will said the *Queensland* would scoop up everything on the bottom if she makes it before us."

"Aye."

"I don't know why I did it. I wanted to show you — you and Mike Moore..."

"I know, boy." In the half-light Jimmy saw the gentleness of Big Simon's smile. "Try to sleep now."

Jimmy watched the night sky shifting and drifting above him. His ankle was hot and throbbing but, in spite of it, he felt strangely peaceful. Tomorrow? No use to worry about it now. He lay very still. One more thing to be said, that *had* to be said.

"Thanks. Thanks, Big Simon."

Big Simon nodded.

The words were out and it hadn't been so hard after all, after the start. Jimmy closed his eyes. He was very tired and now he could sleep.

8

"Tide's turned." Big Simon shook Jimmy's shoulder. "We've got to get back."

Jimmy opened his eyes and was strangely wide awake at once. He sat up carefully, mindful of the hot, stabbing pain in his ankle.

Big Simon was slicing chunks from the smoked ham. He held a piece toward Jimmy on the point of his knife, a fish knife with a sawtooth edge.

Jimmy took the meat, then looked around. The moon had paled to a white shadow and the sky was a luminous gray, the color of day beginning. He scanned the ice. Nothing had changed. Floe after floe piled between them and the shore and he saw Big Simon's dory, at least a quarter of a mile away, high on a knobby pan, the outboard tilted on its stern.

He moved a little and pain jarred him again.

"When you and Captain Will talked about taking a dory to Eagle Rock, you meant using a motor?" he asked.

Big Simon nodded. "For sure. And, even then, not against an outgoing tide." He lifted the blankets off Jimmy's legs and touched his ankle. "Hurt bad?"

"A bit," Jimmy said, and Big Simon nodded again. He stripped off the socks and unwound the red handkerchief. "Take a look." Jimmy sat straighter and peered down.

His ankle and foot were purple-red, the skin puffed and shiny.

"It's not...it's not frostbite," he stammered. His mind grappled with amputation, the sound of a saw going through the bone.

"No." Big Simon shook his head. "I've seen enough of that to know it. Had it myself once. Lost two of my toes. You've got a sprain, a bad one, and the color's from bruising — contusion, they call it."

Relieved, Jimmy lay back. I know nothing about Big Simon, he thought, and then he thought again. I know everything about him, everything important, but nothing about how it was for him before. "You lost two toes?" he asked. "When was this?"

Big Simon retired the handkerchief. "Oh, a few

years back, up on Great Bear Lake. I was working with a company mining uranium. My snowmobile got into trouble. I was on the ice all night and part of the next day. That's right on the Circle, up there." He lifted Jimmy's leg and pulled on the socks. "Try standing. I'll give you a hand."

Jimmy steadied himself on Big Simon's shoulder. The second he put his weight to the ankle pain flared along his leg, up to his thigh. He gasped and bit his lip.

"Bad, huh?"

Jimmy tried to speak. Waves of sickness washed over him.

"Sit back down." Big Simon scratched his head, turned his back to Jimmy and looked across the ice.

Jimmy eased himself back in the dory. He felt helpless, hopeless. How would they get off the ice if he couldn't even stand?

"I'm going to look around," Big Simon said at last, and Jimmy nodded. He watched Big Simon leap to the other floe. He looked beyond him to the opening of the inlet, the smooth roundness of the top of Eagle's Rock. What were they doing now, back on the *Kathleen II*? He pictured Captain Will standing in the wheelhouse, the old pipe in his teeth, ranting and raging over losing his nets and taking a boy on the voyage, a boy who left his watch and took a dory without permission.

Even if he *had* liked the boy's father! Jimmy blinked. Ranting and raging on the outside, bad hurting inside and feeling as helpless and hopeless as Jimmy felt. And what if the other two boats left while Captain Will watched them go?

Jimmy pulled himself as high as he could and looked toward shore. There was still little open water. The tide that had carried him out had not cleared the main body of the pack from the in-lying sea. Maybe the *Daughter Dear* and the *Queensland* would be stuck where they were for a while. He found that he had clenched his teeth and that he was thinking *please, please, please* the way he always did when things were bad and he had no way to make them better.

"There's a narrow lead on the other side of this pan," Big Simon called. He jumped across. "It's too tight for the oars, but if we can get the dory over and into the water we could scull her. Get her around to where I hauled the other one." He looked at Jimmy. "I'd best pull the dory, then come back and help you. I'd carry you if I could, but the ice edges won't hold the both of us. You'll have to make the jump yourself. It's going to hurt. Can you do it?"

Simon's eyes, Jimmy noticed, were the exact color of the sea behind him.

"Can you?"

Jimmy swallowed. "Aye," he said.

Strange eyes, deep and clear under the rust-red brows. "I thought you could."

He took Jimmy's boot from the boat and sliced it down the length and over the foot, his stroke as smooth as that of a splitter opening a cod.

Jimmy eased his foot into the boot and Big Simon pulled the rubber edges together. He frowned. "That's not much good."

"Maybe the potato sack," Jimmy suggested.

"Aye." Big Simon emptied out the food and put the sack over the ripped boot. "Still not great," he muttered, tying the string around and around the sack, "but it'll have to do."

He helped Jimmy out of the dory. "When I drag her off the floe, the ice'll heave like a sick whale." He wedged the oars in the ice, blade down. "Hold on to these. I don't want you down when the water comes over."

There was an ice knob, nine or ten inches high, and he lifted Jimmy's hurt foot onto it. "Keep it up here if you can. With luck it'll stay dry."

Jimmy stood tensed, the butt end of an oar under each armpit. The fear-pain was back in his stomach, floating down, meeting and mingling with the pain in his ankle.

Big Simon pushed at the dory, his weight to the back of it. Every few inches he stopped and lifted it over humps and hollows. When they got close to the edge the ice pan began dipping.

Jimmy waited. He saw Big Simon take the tow rope. The ice was slippery at the edge and he held his breath, seeing how the sea came over Big Simon's feet, although he was still four or five yards from the rim.

Then Big Simon took a splashing, awkward run, and he was leaping the gap that came as their floe went down, leaping up and over. The tow rope jerked and Jimmy saw the dory gather speed and jump behind Big Simon so that it looked as though it would crash into him, knock him over as it had knocked Jimmy over earlier.

Under him the pan bucked and swayed and he had no way to see what was happening on the other floe. Ice water swirled around his leg and ran off as quickly as it had come. He staggered, but he was still up and the sea had not reached his torn boot. That much was all right. The pan still rocked, but the water flowed away before it reached him.

He saw Big Simon, feet braced, straining at the tow rope. The dory was halfway up on the new ice, its stern in the water between the floes, the old floe holding it wedged. As he looked, his pan rose and Big Simon heaved. The dory slid up and toward him. Jimmy saw the remains of the ham roll out over the back, and the plastic bottle too, and then something else. Something dull and green that dropped with a splash into the black water and disappeared as the floes joined and closed over it.

He stood very still, his eyes on the ice. The tackle box. No way to get it. Gone. Gone forever. There was a stretched ache under his ears, like a stitched wound.

Big Simon had the dory high on the floe and stood, panting, beside it. "Hold tight, Jimmy. I'm coming back."

In a couple of minutes he was beside him. His voice was low. "Boy, I'm sorry about the tackle box."

Jimmy spoke through the tightness of the stitched wound on each side of his jaw. "It was my dad's."

"I know." Big Simon put out a freckled hand, then drew it back. "If there was a way to get it back..."

"There's no way. What's gone is gone."

"Aye. And we have to move on. That's always the way it is." He swung Jimmy up and gave him the oars. "I'll carry you. You take these."

When Big Simon put him down they were so close to the edge that the pan hung at a slant. Big Simon took the oars. "I'll reach one of these across to you. Grab a hold when you can. It'll help some."

Jimmy stood, balanced on his good leg, waiting.

"Now, Jimmy. Come."

He took a shuffling step. The pain moved with

him, stabbing, flashing like light, and it was more than he could bear, more than anyone could bear. But he had to. Big Simon was calling him, and it was important that he go to him, for he had never gone before. But Big Simon had come to him and now he was calling him. He took another step, and the oar was there, wavering, but *there*, and he grabbed it and put his weight on his bad ankle for the jump so that he would land on his good one. He was throwing himself forward, and the scream was his scream, a scream like an angry gull, a fighting gull, a wounded gull, and Big Simon was catching him. For an instant he saw the terrible tenderness on Big Simon's face and heard the terrible gentleness in his voice, and then the pain took over, flooding, drowning, covering, and then there was nothing but darkness.

Big Simon was sculling the dory.

Jimmy lay on the bottom and looked up, past the length of the fisherman's boots, the legs in the wool trousers, the pea coat that had buttons with anchors on them. The big, freckled hand was firm on the oar. The light gray eyes in the totem-pole face stared straight ahead.

Jimmy smiled. "Hi," he said.

He was proud of his smile and his easy voice. His ankle ticked, like a hot heartbeat, and the strings that held the sack to his boot were all at once tight, too tight. He bent to loosen them.

Big Simon looked down. "You did fine."

Jimmy squirmed himself up and saw how low the dory lay in the water. Ice pans shoved them as they slipped slowly by and there was no sound but the soft swish of the paddle moving back and forth behind, pushing them on.

Big Simon shipped the oar and they glided to the edge of the knobby floe that held the other dory. He took the tow rope and stepped cautiously up onto the pan.

Jimmy watched him tie the tow rope to his belt and move across the ice, the rope snaking behind him. The shore was closer now, definitely closer, with the floes packed loosely between here and the cliffs. Jimmy looked up at the sky. Full daylight, and there were leads now, lots of leads. ... As though he were there, he saw the *Daughter Dear* and the *Queensland*, weighing anchor, readying to go. He looked quickly toward the Inlet, but the sea was empty except for its load of floating ice. He saw nothing, but still he knew. The knowing was in him, gut deep.

Big Simon was coming, pushing the other dory into the water, jumping into it, lowering the outboard. He fastened the rope to a ring on his dory stern and secured it.

Above them the sky was growing brighter, but a layer of fog, smoke-gray, crept in low on the horizon. Big Simon nodded toward it.

"That'll help keep them in McKenzie for a while, I'm thinking."

Jimmy felt the tightness in his face relax and he grinned. *Thanks, thanks*, he thought, the way he always did when the bad eased.

"Did you know I'm to be captain of the *Kathleen II* on her next voyage?" Big Simon asked. His voice was almost shy and he didn't look at Jimmy as he bent over the starter cord and pulled at the motor.

"Captain?" Jimmy began, remembering things he had heard without understanding. "Will you..." He stopped. Over Big Simon's shoulder he saw something. A boat was nosing northward out of the Inlet. He saw the single mast, the high blunt bow, the deckhouse aft of midships.

"Look!" he yelled. "The *Queensland*!" His voice was almost lost in the starting roar of the motor. He pointed as Big Simon turned.

"She's going to make a run for the berths, to try to beat the fog," Big Simon shouted.

Jimmy groaned. My fault, he thought. Captain Will would be trying for it too, if it weren't for me.

The *Queensland* moved delicately, picking her way through the heavy, drifting ice.

Jimmy cupped his hands around his mouth to throw the words over the noise between them. "Could we get there before her?"

Big Simon opened the throttle and the motor

roared. His teeth flashed in a grin under the rust-red mustache. "We just might. She's bigger. There's a lot of ice. She'll need to go easy."

The front dory picked up speed and the second one hissed through the sea behind it, water rising like wings from its bows.

"Hold tight," Big Simon yelled, and Jimmy lay back. His ankle hurt, hurt bad, and it would be a while until he could get it seen to. But they would get there first, after all, and maybe it was partly because of him. Because he'd been stupid, he reminded himself, and nearly been killed and nearly ruined it for everybody. But still.... They had no water and little food, but the captain of the *Queensland* wouldn't let them want. All things together, he felt pretty good.

They were coming in on the cliffs, weaving through the floes, their course true and steady for Eagle's Rock.

The *Queensland* had stopped in the ice and, as he watched, he saw her reverse and try another lead. The maze, Jimmy thought, the maze with the prize at the end — and he and Big Simon were leading, heading for the box marked COD HERE. He began to hum under his breath the song Old Taylor had been singing on the night watch.

> *Ye finny monsters of the deep,*
> *Lift up your heads and shout!*

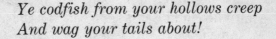

Ye codfish from your hollows creep
And wag your tails about!

He let his mind shift to the green tackle box lying in the dark under the floating islands of ice and he was filled with a gentle sadness. Good-bye, Dad, he thought. I'll remember. They say I'm like you, and that's good, but I have to let you go and move on. I guess Mother does too. You understand.

Behind them the *Queensland* sounded her horn in a mournful moan. The fog was moving in, blotting out the world, filling the sky. Through the drift of it he saw above them the painted yellow eye of the eagle.

Jimmy smiled. He looked at Big Simon, his back straight and strong, bigger than any back in the world. Captain Simon! No, Captain Big Simon! They'd done it. What he couldn't do alone, they'd done together. It was, in some strange way, a forecast of the future.